THIS BOOK BELONGS TO

PETTICOAT PIRATES

Petticoat
PIRATES

*The Mermaids
of Starfish Reef*

ERICA-JANE WATERS

www.lbkids.co.uk

LITTLE, BROWN BOOKS FOR YOUNG READERS

First published in Great Britain in 2013 by Little, Brown Books for Young Readers

A CIP catalogue record for this book
is available from the British Library.

ISBN 978-1-907411-96-0

Typeset in Golden Cockerill by M Rules
Printed and bound in Great Britain by
Clays, St Ives plc

Papers used by LBYR are from well-managed forests
and other responsible sources.

MIX
Paper from
responsible sources
FSC
www.fsc.org   FSC® C104740

Little, Brown Books for Young Readers
An imprint of
Little, Brown Book Group
100 Victoria Embankment
London EC4Y 0DY

An Hachette UK Company
www.hachette.co.uk

www.lbkids.co.uk

For Nick, thank-you for your never-ending support

SCALLOP BAY

STARFISH REEF

RAZOR BAY

WHIRLPOOL GULLY

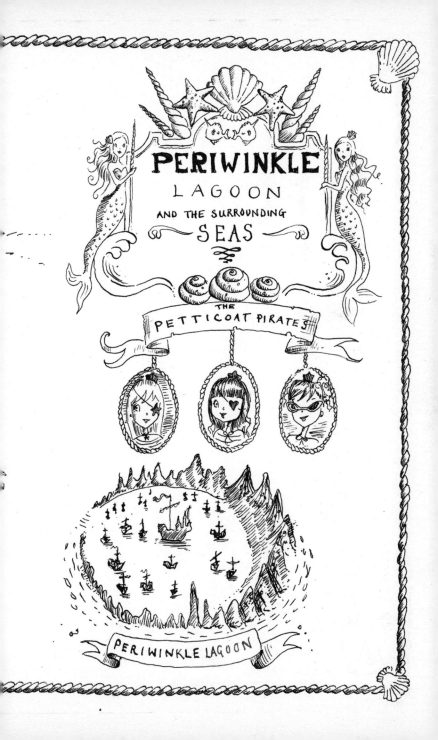

PERIWINKLE
LAGOON
AND THE SURROUNDING
SEAS

THE
PETTICOAT PIRATES

PERIWINKLE LAGOON

Contents

Prologue

"What are they?" said one pirate.

"Can we eat 'em?" asked another.

"They smell funny," said a third.

A large group of pirates had gathered around a small basket shaded from the sun by a tattered umbrella. The basket had floated into Periwinkle Lagoon early this summer morning.

"Away, pirates," came the stern voice of Captainess Periwinkle. "I'll take care of this!"

The beautiful Captainess leant over the basket and peeled back the soft pink blanket that was embroidered with a heart, a starfish and a seahorse.

"Babies!" declared Captainess Periwinkle. "Three pirate-girl babies!"

She scooped the tiny creatures up in her arms, holding them tightly against her pearl necklaces.

"I don't know where you came from, me hearties, but you came here to me at Periwinkle Lagoon. I will care for you as if you are my own, and teach you how to be good and true pirates."

The three babies were named Marina, Aqua and Oceana, and Captainess Periwinkle was true to her word.

Ten pirate years later, they came to have their own ship: *The Petticoat.*

They called themselves the Petticoat Pirates.

MARINA

BABY MARINA

AQUA

BABY AQUA

OCEANA

BABY OCEANA

Chapter One

The salty sea air blew through Marina's ink-black hair as she waited for her shipmates, Oceana and Aqua, to arrive.

Sitting on the deck of her ship, *The Petticoat*, she watched as all the other ships in Periwinkle Lagoon gently bobbed up and down in the warm blue waters. She cupped her hands around her mug of hot kelp tea and felt happy and safe. The cliffs of the little lagoon stretched around her like strong arms,

protecting her from the perils that lay in the vast seas beyond.

"Marina," came a loud voice from below, "throw me the rope ladder. I'm hanging on like a limpet down here."

It was Aqua. She was struggling with a large pile of leather-bound books, her wrists jingle-jangling with gold, silver and pearl bracelets. Aqua spent many long hours tucked up in her bunk reading and was Periwinkle Lagoon's resident sea beastie expert. But as much as Aqua loved books and sea monsters, she equally loved fashion. Her colourful skirts and extravagant hats were often the talk of the lagoon.

"You're back early," said Marina. She lowered a rickety rope ladder down the starboard side of *The Petticoat*'s hull. "I thought you'd be at the library ship all day long!"

"No use trying to concentrate, it was far too noisy and busy," replied Aqua, huffing. She seemed out of breath from climbing a ladder whilst holding so many books. "Just as I arrived, the *Barnacle Babies* nursery boat docked up. I couldn't hear myself think for tiny pirates jibbering and jabbering. I thought I'd be able to concentrate better on these new sea monster books in my cabin."

Marina took one of the books from Aqua as she clambered aboard. She ran her milky white hand over the turtle leather that bound the book.

"May I?" she asked.

"You may, me hearty," replied Aqua, hoisting herself and her many sparkly, sequinned skirts up on to the ship's rail.

Marina undid the brass starfish clasp that kept the thick book closed. She turned the

sand-coloured pages, admiring the beautiful illustrations inside. There were pictures of mermaids, mermen, long serpent-like sea monsters, beautiful sea fairies and various other kinds of magical sea creatures.

"Oh, Aqua, this book is gorgeous," sighed Marina.

"It's a pretty good one," shrugged Aqua, "but I can't wait to get stuck into that beauty!" She gestured with her lacy cuff to an enormous green book at the bottom of her pile. "I found it right at the back of the library ship. It was completely wedged in behind lots of old issues of *Whale Watchers Weekly*."

Marina lifted her eyepatch up on to her forehead and read aloud the golden letters on the spine: *"Very, Very, Very Deep Sea Beasties."*

Aqua's bracelets and bangles jangled as she jumped down on to the deck next to Marina and leant in close to her friend.

"There is very little known about the creatures that live in deep waters, you see. Nobody has ever been able to dive down that far. Well . . . " Aqua paused, "there have been a few research expeditions, but the problem being . . . "

Marina moved in closer to Aqua. "The problem being what?" she asked.

Aqua looked out to the deep seas beyond the lagoon, her blue eyes narrowing. "The problem being that the expeditions never return. I heard that the last one came to a very,

very sticky end. Stickier than a jellyfish's sticky bits!"

All of a sudden, there was a loud thud against the hull of *The Petticoat*, followed by hissing and bubbling sounds.

"Blinking barnacles! What was that?" cried Marina.

She jumped up and cautiously peered over the edge of the ship.

"It sounded very much like a giant sea serpent!" shuddered Aqua, looking around for something sharp to fend off the monster. "What else would make such an awful hissing noise?"

A large puff of blue smoke mushroomed up from the sea as Marina turned back to her friend. "It's not a sea serpent, giant or otherwise," she giggled. "But it IS a heap of trouble."

"Oh, limpets!" spluttered Oceana as she clambered aboard *The Petticoat*. She was clutching a small metal box with a big red button on it. "Limpets, limpets, limpets!"

She squelched past Marina and plopped herself down heavily. Her soggy skirts spread out around her on the deck's wooden boards.

"Whatever's happened?" asked Aqua. She was very relieved to see her friend and not an enormous sea monster.

Oceana removed her shoes and emptied them of seawater, small crabs and seaweed. "Well, I've been at the shipyard working on my new invention, the 'easy oar'. The oars row themselves, you see, using this remote control." Oceana held up the dripping wet box.

"It sounds great!" said Marina, looking over her shoulder at the last of Oceana's little wooden

11

rowing boat. It hissed and bubbled beneath the waves. "So what went wrong?"

"Well, I thought I'd 'easy oar' my way over here to get you for the important meeting at the flagship. It was a test run, to see if it needed any tweaks. But all of a sudden, it started rowing really fast, and I couldn't stop it no matter how many times I pressed the red button."

Oceana stared down at her soggy self.

"It overheated, caught fire and I had to abandon ship before it exploded!"

"That'll explain that great big bang, then!" said Aqua.

Marina sat down and put her arm around her friend, not caring that she was getting soggy too. "Oh, Oceana, I'm so sorry."

"Oh, limpets. I'm the most terrible inventor in the history of Periwinkle Lagoon," Oceana

said, drying her mother-of-pearl-rimmed glasses on Marina's petticoat skirts.

"Oceana," replied Marina, "you're just perfect the way you are!"

"UM, excuse me," interrupted Aqua, suddenly remembering what Oceana had said. "WHAT important meeting over at the flagship?"

"Oh, you were at the library ship when the message boat came around. No doubt with your head buried in a sea monster book!" laughed Marina.

Oceana wrung out her socks and hung them on the ship's rigging. "It's something about a disaster down at Starfish Reef. The mermaids there are blowing bubbles about it!"

"It must be very bad if we're being summoned over to the flagship. Captainess

14

Periiwinkle wouldn't make a whale out of a winkle," said Aqua.

"I hope all the mermaids are OK," Marina mused.

"Look," Oceana pointed over to the flagship, which was moored right in the centre of the lagoon, "the calling flag has been hoisted up. It must be time for the meeting!"

Sure enough, dozens of tiny boats were making their way over to the grand flagship. Its red calling flag flapped in the salty breeze.

"Quick, we're going to be late," Aqua said, gathering up her tower of books and disappearing into her cabin.

"I can't go like this, I'm sopping wet!" protested Oceana.

"Well, you haven't got time to get changed now," giggled Marina, ushering her friend over

the edge of *The Petticoat* and down into a small rowing boat. "Here, put these back on – you'll dry off once we're in the warmth of the flagship."

Oceana seated herself in the boat, and Marina sent her socks and shoes clattering down after her.

"Aqua, come on!" called Marina as she lowered herself down the rope into the little boat. "We're going to miss the beginning of the meeting."

"I'm scuttling as fast as my pirate legs will scuttle," Aqua called back. "I just needed my hat. It's as nippy as a baby crab's claw out there tonight."

Marina and Oceana smiled at each other as Aqua settled down next to them. Her neck and wrists were adorned with pearl and shell necklaces and bangles and she wore a large

pearl-encrusted hat, topped off with a peacock feather, upon her blonde locks.

'What!?" Aqua jangled. "A pirate girl likes to look nice for such occasions!"

"Are we all ready?" giggled Marina, taking the heavy wooden oars.

"Just let me get my socks on! And take out this squidgy thing from between my toes!" said Oceana, flicking a sea anemone over the side of the boat.

"I think you're just about presentable now," laughed Marina. As she spoke, she picked a frond of seaweed out of her friend's wavy chestnut hair.

And so the three young Petticoat Pirates rowed their way over to the flagship, anxiously anticipating what news Captainess Periwinkle had to tell them.

Chapter Two

By the time the Petticoat Pirates arrived at the hull of the grand flagship, many tiny boats were moored alongside it, bobbing up and down in the darkening seas.

"Look down there," Marina gasped, pointing below the sea's inky surface. Two parallel rows of glowing jellyfish stretched from the ship's keel right the way across the water to the entrance of the lagoon. "They must be expecting some underwater

visitors – those jellyfish are to guide their path."

"Do you think the mermaids of Starfish Reef are coming?" Oceana asked.

"It must be very serious if the mermaids have come all this way!" replied Marina with a worried look on her face.

Aqua fastened their boat to the side of the great ship and looked around for a rope to climb. "This one will do." She steadied the boat as Marina and Oceana grabbed hold and began to climb towards the deck.

"Great gulls!" gulped Oceana, looking around shyly and pushing her glasses back up her nose. "Look at all these pirates. Maybe I'll just wait for you on *The Petticoat*. I'll row back and pick you up later, and you can tell me all about the meeting then."

"Don't worry, Oceana, don't be nervous," Marina said. She put a reassuring arm around her friend. "Aqua and I will take care of you, and besides, nobody's going to be looking at you – it's Captainess Periwinkle they're here to see."

"Come on, me hearty, how come someone as clever as a catfish's whiskers can be so shy?" said Aqua, who now stood on the deck with her friends. "And you're prettier than a pearl to boot!"

"Thank you," muttered Oceana. Her face turned lobster pink as she stared at her buckled shoes.

"Come on, you two," smiled Marina. "Let's get to this meeting before it's over!"

The girls went down several flights of wooden stairs. The steps twisted their way deep into the bowels of the ship as they headed

towards the grand ballroom on the very bottom deck.

As they pushed open the heavy wooden door, the loud chattering of pirates in the ballroom hit them like a wave.

Marina pushed her way through the crowds towards the front. "This way," she whispered, "we'll be able to see better from over here . . . girls?"

She turned around to see Aqua pulling Oceana by her corset strings towards Marina.

"You can't escape that easily!" laughed Aqua. "Can't you see what a fuss you're making?"

"I can't see anything!" quivered Oceana. "My glasses have steamed up!"

"Oh, Oceana," giggled Marina, "you really don't do crowds, do you!"

They found a space to sit, and Aqua started rummaging in her cape. "I've got something that will cheer you up! Guess what I've got in my pocket?"

"Knowing you, probably a jam jar containing a rare breed of sparkly sea slime!" said Marina.

"Nope, better than that." Aqua pulled out a little blue and white stripy bag with "Periwinkle Deli Stores" written on it in big green letters. "Ta da! I picked up some sugared sea sponge from the market ship while I was out today." She waved the little paper bag under Oceana's nose.

"I can never turn down sugared sea sponge," said Oceana, managing a little smile.

Suddenly, a loud voice came from the front of the room. It was Captainess Periwinkle. "Ahoy, good pirates of Periwinkle Lagoon!"

"Ahoy, Captainess," the room full of pirates shouted in unison, the ceiling above their heads sparkling with hundreds of little glowing starfish.

"I gather you here to share some desperate and dastardly news."

Aqua pointed at the open hatch in the floor at the front of the room. The dark

ocean lapped up around its edges. "Look," she whispered, "there's something moving beneath the surface."

"I have a feeling that the mermaids really have come all the way from Starfish Reef to see us," Marina replied.

"Well, as long as it's not another giant sea cucumber like we had at the last meeting!" Oceana said, her eyes wide with excitement. "I heard it took weeks to clear up the mess!"

All three girls clasped their hands over their mouths to stop themselves giggling out loud.

Captainess Periwinkle stood with one pearl-encrusted boot on a footstool, the other firmly planted on the wooden floorboards. She clutched a golden goblet in one hand, the other hand on her hip. Her blood-red skirt reached the floor and she wore a beautiful

sword engraved with shells and sea serpents on her belt.

"Pirates! Disaster has struck at Starfish Reef. As you know, the farms and gardens of Starfish Reef provide us with all our fresh seafood and vegetables. Without the hard work of the mer-farmers, the store ship would be empty and we would have rumbling bellies."

"Mmmm, sea lettuce salad is my favourite," gushed Aqua.

"Shhhh," hissed Marina, "listen!"

"The crops have been destroyed and the farm creatures have disappeared."

A loud gasp echoed around the ballroom.

"My good friends the chief mermaids of Starfish Reef have travelled for many miles to inform us of this terrifying news. Please welcome Buttonweed, Dulsie and Slokie." Out of the hatch's inky green water surfaced three beautiful mermaids.

Buttonweed was the biggest of the three, her skin tinged green, with shimmering golden scales. Her blonde hair hung down her back and was fastened with seashell clasps. Dulsie's skin was also tinged green, but her scales were silver in colour and she had long white hair that spread around her shoulders. Slokie was the most striking mermaid of the three with golden skin, silky long brown hair and sparkly

pink and gold scales which looked like the sunset.

"Now that is not a giant sea cucumber," said Oceana in astonishment as she gazed at the mermaids.

"Unfortunately," continued Captainess Periwinkle, "I do not speak Mer very well. Is there any pirate here who can translate?"

The ballroom was silent until Marina stepped forward and said, "Yes, Captainess, I can speak fluent Mer."

"Then please make your way to the front," gestured Captainess Periwinkle.

Nervously Marina made her way through the crowd of pirates towards the three sea creatures. They were poised effortlessly and gracefully on the edges of the ocean hatch.

Captainess Periwinkle leant towards

Marina, close enough that the Petticoat Pirate could smell her sea strawberry perfume.

"I have only been able to understand a little of what these magnificent creatures are tryin' to say," whispered Captainess Periwinkle. "I'm as grateful as a shark in a shoal of sardines to yer."

"It's my pleasure," Marina blushed.

The mermaid at the front began to speak. She made the most beautiful liquid sound, like the trickle of crystal-clear water. Marina started to translate for the entranced crowd.

"I am Buttonweed and I'm sorry to bring such worrying news. We suspect that a large beast swam up from the deep under the shadow of night and deliberately destroyed our farms. The coral walls that pen in the sea snail herds have been completely shattered."

"But who or what could it be?" asked Captainess Periwinkle.

Marina translated these words back to the mermaid. This time Slokie replied, and Marina listened carefully then spoke again to the crowd.

"We do not know, but we did find these large glittering scales amongst what was left of the sugar kelp."

The third mermaid, Dulsie, held up two enormous scales the size of dinner plates and showed them to the pirates.

An uproar broke out in the great ship as the pirates began to panic.

"It's a monster fish, with teeth as big as cannons," one shouted.

"It's an electric eel as long as this ship," cried another.

"QUIET, PIRATES!" shouted Captainess Periwinkle. "Please settle yourselves. These fine mermaids have come to us for help and we must remain calm. Now, does anyone in Periwinkle Lagoon recognise these enormous scales? Aqua, you are our resident expert in mysteries of the deep – do you know to whom they belong?"

Aqua choked on her sugared sea sponge and felt the eyes of a thousand pirates burning into her.

"Yes, Captainess," she replied. "I know the sea beast to whom they belong."

Chapter Three

"Please Aqua, please come hither," Captainess Periwinkle said, gesturing to a space next to Marina.

The sweaty crowd of pirates parted as Aqua made her way towards Captainess Periwinkle, Marina and the three mermaids.

Aqua felt a tug at her lacy sleeve as an old pirate stopped her.

"Is it a big sea monster, Aqua?"

"Does it have sharp, poisonous claws?" asked another, her black teeth chattering.

"I bet it has teeth as long as my wooden leg!" cried a third pirate as the room erupted into a sea-monster panic.

"It'll be coming for us next – we'll all be eaten come the morn!"

"SILENCE!" Captainess Periwinkle shouted again at her unruly pirates. "This young pirate has been an expert on mysteries of the deep since she were a nipper. Listen and learn!"

Aqua swallowed hard. "Well," she began,

"I do believe that these scales belong to the Nori, a giant mermaid that resides deep, deep beneath the waves by Starfish Reef."

The pirates all gathered closer to hear what Aqua was saying.

"No one has seen the Nori for many a year, but it is believed she still exists down in her dark, watery home. She only ever comes out to feed at night, and has never been sighted during the day."

"What does she feed *on*?" asked a quivering pirate at the front.

"She has a huge appetite, eating anything and everything that crosses her path!" Aqua replied excitedly. "She will suck up whole shoals of fish. It has even been

rumoured that she could gobble up a mermaid in one big bite!"

Marina, standing next to Aqua, gave her friend a sharp nudge and tilted her head to the mermaids.

"Oh, I'm sorry," Aqua said, turning towards Buttonweed, Dulsie and Slokie, "I didn't mean to upset you."

The mermaids sighed. They began to speak again.

"They say," translated Marina, "that the Nori must be a creature of vast size, because the damage done could not have been caused by anything smaller than a ship! The crops were ripped out of the seabed with great force and shredded into tiny pieces. They say that if the Nori is not captured then perhaps the mermaids and everyone in Periwinkle Lagoon will . . . "

"Will what, Marina?" asked Captainess Periwinkle. She looked very concerned.

"Will be the Nori's next meal!"

A great din started up in the ballroom. The pirates flung eyepatches and buckled shoes about the place in panic.

"SILENCE YOUR ROWDY PIRATE TONGUES!" Captainess Periwinkle shouted, holding her sword high in the air. "The next pirate to make a sound will be made to walk the plank at Shark Fin Bay! Now out with you all while I deal with this dangerous situation!"

Marina and Aqua began to edge their way back to Oceana, who was still watching nervously from within the crowd.

"Apart from you three! Marina, Aqua, Oceana, you stay behind," Captainess Periwinkle said firmly.

Slowly, the rest of the pirates shuffled out of the grand ballroom, leaving the floor littered with empty goblets and the odd wooden leg.

The ballroom seemed even more beautiful now; the little glowing starfish twinkled even brighter. After the noise of the rabble of pirates had gone, the girls could hear the waves in the ocean hatch gently lapping around the magnificent mermaids.

"My fine Petticoat Pirates, I've a grand favour to ask of ye," continued Captainess Periwinkle.

Marina stepped forward a little. "Captainess, if there's anything we can do, we will gladly help."

Oceana threw Aqua a shivering look. "Anything?"

"Yes," replied Aqua, giving her friend a gentle nudge. "Anything!"

"Marina, you are a fine cartographer. Your

38

detailed maps are legendary within these seas. You are fluent in Mer with a mind as sharp as a razor clam and your wind-

whispering skills are unique and bewitching."

Marina's milky white skin flushed red.

"Aqua, I know more than anyone your knowledge and passion for deep-sea beasties. When you were an infant, you had me read you sea monster tales rather than lullabies at bedtime. You are fearless, both in facing ocean beasts and

in your fashion sense. You know how to slay a sea dragon, and how to look fabulous whilst doing it."

Aqua grinned. She couldn't argue with that!

"Oceana, your studious and methodical nature is most admirable. Your inventive and practical mind is a rare thing in pirate nature. You care deeply for your friends, and your loyalty ensures that no one will ever come to harm under your watch."

The three pirates held their breath, listening anxiously to hear what Captainess Periwinkle would say next.

"It is for these reasons, me hearties, that I am sending you on a mission, deep beneath the waves at Starfish Reef. I want you to find and capture the Nori."

Chapter Four

The sun was just peeking its sleepy head over the cliffs of Periwinkle Lagoon after a long night for the Petticoat Pirates.

Marina yawned and stretched out her arms. "Time for another pot of kelp tea to keep us going, methinks," she said, reaching for the kettle.

"Perfect idea," said Oceana sleepily. "I'm falling asleep at my drawing board here!"

Marina shuffled over to her friend and

looked over her shoulder at the intricate drawing in front of her.

"Oh, Oceana, you are so clever! Is that our capsulette? Captainess Periwinkle will be so proud of you."

"Thank you, Marina. I hope so." Oceana pointed at her drawing with her pencil. "This is what will enable us to travel very, very deep under the sea. It's extra thick glass made from the sand at Oyster Bay. Captainess Periwinkle said I could order any materials I liked, and they will arrive at the shipyard later this morning."

"It's ingenious, and so pretty, too!" said Marina.

"These, just here," Oceana waved her pencil over several little star shapes along the sides of the vessel, "are lights to shine our way in the murky depths of the reef."

The DEEP SEA CAPSULETTE

SIDE VIEW

DASHBOARD AND CONTROLS

"Oh, I utterly adore it, and I know Aqua will too," gushed Marina. "But where has she got to?"

"She popped over to the market ship about twenty minutes ago to fetch some sea strawberry jam for breakfast, while you were asleep on your maps," laughed Oceana.

Marina hopped back over to the map that she'd been plotting through the night. Its yellow corners were held down on the table by four heavy seashells.

"Oh, barnacles! I've dribbled on the corner of Starfish Reef, and the ink's gone all smudgy." She sighed heavily and began rubbing at the mark, her inky fingers only making the stain bigger.

"I'm sure we can navigate around your smudge," giggled Oceana, lifting her head to peer out of the porthole. "At long last! Aqua's back," she said.

Aqua burst in through the cabin door clutching a long, thin loaf of bread and a basket over her arm.

"Great gillyglippers, it's as cold as a crab at Christmas!" she shivered. "Can I smell kelp tea?"

"Just made a fresh pot," said Marina, setting out three oyster shell teacups and saucers on the table along with three large oyster shell plates.

"Don't make any more smudges on your map," warned Oceana as she anxiously watched Marina pouring the kelp tea.

"I'll be careful, don't fret!" she replied.

The three pirates all sat down around the table in their cosy cabin, sipping their tea and feasting on sea strawberry jam on toast.

As soon as she'd swallowed her last mouthful, Aqua spoke. "I've been researching all night and it seems that the Nori is even BIGGER, and even MORE terrifying than any of us ever imagined!"

Marina leant over and put some more driftwood on the wood burner. "Exactly HOW big and HOW terrifying are we talking?" she asked.

Aqua jumped up from her chair and disappeared into her cabin. She re-emerged holding a book so big she could hardly carry it, and thumped it down on the table, making the teacups jump off their saucers. Then she flung open the book to a page she had marked with a seagull feather.

The Petticoat Pirates stared at the picture before them. There, on the page, was a

painting of a large green mermaid. However, to call her a mermaid sounded too nice, for this was NOT a mermaid, this was a monster! And in beautiful swirly writing below the creature were the words:

THE NORI.

"Limpets . . . " squeaked Oceana, barely able to make a noise.

"Limpets doesn't really cover it," Marina squeaked back. She ran her finger softly over the illustration, imagining that the picture itself might bite. "Look at her teeth," she said, pointing at the rows and rows of pointy yellow teeth inside the Nori's mouth.

"And look at her hands!" shrieked Oceana. "And her n-n-n-nails."

"Those aren't nails, my little catfish, those are claws – poisonous claws! One scratch from the Nori and there'll be no more sitting about drinking kelp tea." Aqua leant back in her chair, her hands behind her head. "We need to catch this beast before it destroys all of Starfish Reef and beyond."

"You're right, Aqua," Marina said. She stood up and put her hands on her hips. "Captainess Periwinkle has chosen us to save Starfish Reef, and in turn Periwinkle Lagoon. We must be brave. We must not let anybody perish."

"Absolutely – we must be brave and go forth on our mission," Oceana added, placing her trembling teacup and saucer back on the table.

She un-taped her designs from her drawing board, rolled them up and pulled on her heavy cloak. "The glass from Oyster Bay will have arrived at the shipyard by now. I'll be back this evening with the capsulette."

"I'll pack some food and essentials ready for your return," Aqua called out as her friend climbed down the hull of *The Petticoat* and into the rowing boat.

Marina packed up her ink, nibs and a roll of paper. "I'm going to meet Dulsie, Slokie and Buttonweed. They're going to help me plot the route to Starfish Reef," she said.

As Marina stepped out on to the chilly deck of *The Petticoat*, her tummy became

tight and it felt as though it were filled with a thousand wriggling black eels.

"We will capture the Nori," she whispered to herself. "We will be brave."

Chapter Five

The shadows in Periwinkle Lagoon were becoming longer as the daylight slipped away. Marina and Aqua were peering out of a porthole, anxiously watching for Oceana to return with the capsulette.

"I do believe I can see her bubbling her way over now!" Aqua suddenly said excitedly.

The girls rushed out onto deck. Over on the other side of the lagoon they could just make out a light sparkling under the waves.

It moved slowly towards them, a trail of little bubbles spraying out behind. The small vessel soon surfaced alongside *The Petticoat*'s stern, its white lights dimming as it did so.

The top of the deep-sea capsulette opened slowly with a hiss, revealing a very happy Oceana. "It's finished," she beamed, unable to contain her pride. "I designed something that actually works!"

"Oh, Oceana, it's gorgeous," Marina said. She looked in admiration at the pearlescent pink paintwork and pretty star-shaped lights.

"Well, it was Captainess Periwinkle's shipbuilders who did most of the work," Oceana said, a little embarrassed by her friend's compliment.

"Oceana!" piped up Aqua as she helped to tether the capsulette to the ship. "You're as silly as a squid in a skirt! YOU and only YOU designed this magnificent piece of machinery – building it is the easy bit!"

Just then, the three beautiful mermaids surfaced next to the capsulette. It was Slokie who spoke to the girls with her liquid sound, as her long brown hair flowed around her.

"She says," translated Marina, "that we must hurry. Who knows the damage a

dangerous sea monster like the Nori could have done by now."

"Then anchors aweigh!" cried Aqua. The girls quickly took their places aboard *The Petticoat*. Marina took the wheel, Aqua hoisted the sails and Oceana climbed up the rigging to the crow's nest at the top of the mast and they sailed quietly and speedily out of Periwinkle Lagoon, the three mermaids swimming alongside the ship.

Almost as soon as the moon had risen in the starry sky, it was covered up by thick black

storm clouds. Marina stood on the deck of their ship, listening to the words of the wind and studying her map.

"Brrr . . . where did our friend the moon go?" asked Aqua, shuffling over to Marina.

Oceana joined them. "How far to the reef?" she asked with a shiver.

"Well, according to the map we've just got to get past the rocks of Razor Bay, but I can't tell how close they are without the stars or moon. I think I need to ask the wind to guide us," replied Marina.

Marina let down her dark hair, allowing it to blow in the wind.

"What is it, Marina? Is the wind telling you something?" asked Oceana.

"Shivering shellfish," said Aqua. "You give me the collywobbles when you speak with the wind!"

"Shhhh!" whispered Marina. "I'm trying to listen."

The girls stood very still as the wind whipped around their faces. The dark clouds above began to move, letting the moon shine through to light up their way. Oceana and Aqua held their breath and waited for Marina to speak again.

"There will be a great wind blowing from the east, so we must enter Razor Bay from the west. That way, we'll be sailing into the wind. If we have the wind behind us we will be pushed straight into the jagged rocks and be wrecked."

Marina's prediction quickly came true. A strong gale began to blow, and the sky was lit up by flashes of lightning. *The Petticoat* moved closer to Razor Bay where the mermaids were waiting.

"To get past these rocks we need to move into position," Marina said, taking charge of the Petticoat Pirates. "Aqua, crawl as far along the bowsprit as you can so you can see the rocks. I want you to shout 'starboard' or 'port' depending on which way I should steer *The Petticoat.*"

"Yes, Capt'n!" shouted Aqua. She began shimmying along the pole that stuck out at the front of their ship.

"Oceana," continued Marina, "I need you to control the sails so we can slow down or speed up as need be."

"Yes, Capt'n," replied Oceana as she climbed into position on the ship's rigging.

Slowly and steadily *The Petticoat* wound its way around the razor-sharp rocks, its path being lit by the mermaids' algae friends.

"PORT, PORT, PORT!" Aqua began shouting wildly, barely able to cling on in the wind. "STEER PORT!!!"

The Petticoat's wooden hull scraped along the edge of a rock, making a terrifying thunderous noise.

"We've hit a rock!" Aqua continued to shout over the thunder and the rain and the wind. "We're going to sink!"

Marina looked up to Oceana, who was trying to control *The Petticoat*'s wide sails as they flapped violently in the wind. "Oceana, we've hit a rock! I need you to grab your tools and patch

up the hole in the hull from the inside." Marina's wet, inky hair stuck to her face as she shouted.

"Limpets!" shouted Oceana. She dashed below deck and *The Petticoat* sailed on.

"STARBOARD, MORE STARBOARD!" cried Aqua. The rocks became a little further apart as they edged near the exit to the reef.

Marina turned the wheel frantically, following Aqua's guidance. Eventually they sailed back into open water. She sighed with relief and waved to Buttonweed, Slokie and Dulsie, who dived beneath the waves to make their way home to Starfish Reef.

"You steered us straight into a rock!" howled Aqua as she climbed back on to deck. "And now we have a hole in our hull!"

"I was following your directions," Marina snapped back.

A very soggy and flustered-looking Oceana emerged from the decks below.

"It wasn't as bad as it sounded. I've fixed it."

"We wouldn't have a hole of any sort if someone hadn't STEERED US INTO A ROCK," Aqua continued, stroppily.

"The important thing is we're all in one piece," Oceana said. She stepped in between her feuding friends.

"I'm sorry, Aqua, but I couldn't hear you over all the rain and wind. I didn't sail us into that rock on purpose," Marina said, her hands on her hips.

"Well, I suppose it was louder than a walrus' whistle, so it must have been hard to hear," Aqua said, unusually quiet. "Anyone fancy getting out of this horrible howling wind and having a nice cup of kelp tea?"

The girls laughed and headed below deck, Marina and Aqua arm in arm. They threw off their wet cloaks and hung them by the wood burner to dry.

"I think we should anchor here for the night," Marina said, sitting down at the table.

"Me too," said Oceana. She passed the dried sugar kelp to Aqua, who was warming some water for the tea. "I'm so tired after all that drama."

"I don't care if I never see a razor rock again!" giggled Aqua.

"The best thing we can do now is get some rest," replied Marina warmly. "We'll set off for Starfish Reef first thing in the morning."

So the anchor was lowered, and as the storm passed over, all was calm in *The Petticoat* once more. But the girls didn't sleep very well

64

that night because despite the still waters, their thoughts and dreams were filled with the yellow teeth and poisonous claws of the Nori.

Chapter Six

Crystal clear water lapped gently around *The Petticoat*'s hull as the three girls arrived at Starfish Reef. It was instantly recognisable from its star-shaped light blue outline under the waves where the water was shallowest. The sea grew darker blue in colour at the centre of the star, where the reef dipped down and the ocean became very, very deep. No one ever ventured there. It was where the pirates believed the Nori would be lurking.

"Oh, just look at it," gushed Oceana. "It's so beautiful here."

"It may look beautiful on the surface," replied Marina, "but we all know that below the waves lies a very, very, very deep sea beastie."

"The sooner we get our eyepatches underwater, the better," said Aqua, already making her way along the deck towards the stern.

"I'll ready the deep-sea capsulette," Oceana said, following Aqua towards the back of *The Petticoat*.

Aqua and Marina lowered the little capsulette into the waves and Oceana lifted the door at the top and climbed inside.

"I just need to make sure the oxygen tank is full and the lights are fully charged."

Marina and Aqua smiled as they watched their clever friend flicking switches and pressing buttons. The panel in front of Oceana flickered with pink and purple lights.

"Right, it's ready," Oceana smiled. "Climb in."

Marina pulled the heavy lid shut above them.

Slowly, Oceana steered the tiny round vessel down under the surface of the water using two little levers.

The waters around the reef were a sight to behold. There were fish in every shade of pink, orange and yellow and they seemed to glow in the warm sunrays shining down from above. Hundreds of tiny orange and red starfish clung to the sides of the rocks. It was these that gave the reef its name.

The girls were startled by a gentle knocking on the side of the capsulette. It was Dulsie.

"Look, she's gesturing for us to follow her," said Marina.

Oceana carefully moved the capsulette deeper down the outside of the reef following Dulsie's lead. It left a little trail of sparkly bubbles behind them. Soon they had reached the flat planes of the seabed and the scene of all the destruction.

Dulsie gestured towards the sugar kelp and pepper dulse fields, completely bare except for a few little straggly strips of seaweed. She glided off again, her long golden green tail moving elegantly in the water.

"Look over there," Aqua pointed. "That must be where they kept the sea snail herds."

Sure enough, Dulsie had swum down to an empty paddock, its intricate coral walls smashed to pieces.

"What's Dulsie pointing at?" Oceana asked, sailing the little vessel carefully down to where the mermaid was hovering.

She moved a lever to shine one of the capsulette's lights down on to the seabed.

"There, look!" Marina said excitedly. "It's one of the Nori's scales."

Shimmering in the blue light was a dinner-plate-sized scale.

Dulsie pointed again.

"I think she wants us to go this way," Oceana said, steering the capsulette in the direction of Dulsie's golden arm.

"Shiver me timbers!" Aqua shouted. "There's another of the scales!"

Dulsie nodded and left the girls to follow the trail of scales.

"I don't think the mermaids will come any closer to the centre of the reef," Marina said as she watched the frightened-looking mermaid swimming away.

The pirates followed the scales back up over the top of the reef and towards the dark

73

interior. They stared over the edge, down into the indigo water.

"Are you telling me that we have to go down there?" shivered Oceana.

"Well, it seems that way. That's where the scales lead to, and that is where the Nori is rumoured to live," replied Aqua, her face pale.

"We're on our own from here," said Marina. "Are we ready?"

The girls looked at one another.

"This is it!" said Aqua, fastening her eyepatch over her eye.

Oceana flicked some switches on the capsulette's control board. "Oxygen tanks full, and ready to go."

The three girls joined hands.

"To the Petticoat Pirates!" they whispered, giving each other's hands a tight squeeze.

"Let's go and catch that sea monster!" Marina said bravely, and Oceana steered the little capsulette off towards the dark hole in the middle of the reef.

Chapter Seven

As Oceana guided the capsulette further down into the depths of the reef, the scene around them changed. Instead of orange and red glowing starfish and brightly coloured coral, the pirates started to see strange underwater creatures.

"Look at that fish!" exclaimed Aqua. "It

looks like a miniature version of our capsulette!"

A round, pale pink little fish looked in at them through the window.

"He's even got his own light!" Marina giggled, admiring the long frond protruding out of the top of the fish's body. The frond had a little blue light on the end.

"We're nearly at the bottom of the reef now," Oceana said in a serious tone, looking at her dials and gauges.

"With any luck we'll land right on top of that Nori's head and knock her out, clean cold!" Aqua added. Her bangles jangled as she shook a pointed finger.

Oceana slowed the capsulette down and they glided gently to the bottom of the reef.

Marina consulted her map. "If we head due

north we'll go through the Red Seaweed Forest. Nobody knows what's in there, so I'm guessing that's where we'll find the Nori's lair."

The girls leant forward to look out of the capsulette window. There was now no sign of life; the only light was that coming from the capsulette.

"It's as eerie as an eel down here," whispered Aqua.

The pirates continued through the darkness, the capsulette's lights shining out on to the vast rippled seabed in front of them.

"There," Marina said suddenly, her nose pressed against the glass. "I see the Red Seaweed Forest!"

The girls glided slowly towards the towering red and purple fronds of seaweed that made up the Red Seaweed Forest.

"Hmmm," Oceana murmured, looking at the radar on her control board, "it looks like there's some kind of large rocky area up ahead."

"Let's go and investigate," Marina said. The long, thick seaweed trunks slowly swayed as they sailed past.

Suddenly the capsulette jolted to a halt, sending the three pirates tumbling forward.

"What the flippers was that?" Aqua shouted, rubbing her arm and re-adjusting her eyepatch.

"We must be stuck in one of the seaweed branches," said Marina. She quickly straightened her petticoats and clambered back up into her seat.

"I don't think WE'RE stuck," Oceana said in a worried tone, "I think something is stuck on us . . . HOLD ON TIGHT!"

A long, pale purple tentacle slithered around the glass of the capsulette, its dark red suckers sticking like glue.

"Limpets," Oceana cried. "It's a giant octopus!"

"Quick, get us out of here!" shouted Marina. "Go up – up!"

"I can't!" Oceana said, out of breath. "Its tentacles are too strong – I can't break us free!"

"So we were worried about a monstrous mermaid, and end up being dinner for an oversized squid instead!" said Aqua. She had her arms outstretched, bracing herself against the walls of the capsulette. "How embarrassing. This is no way for a pirate to go!"

The tiny underwater vessel lurched left and then right as the giant octopus flung it about like a child's toy.

"Limpets, limpets, limpets," Oceana muttered, struggling in vain with the controls.

Marina clung on tightly to her chair, wishing with all her heart that she was safely back on her beloved *Petticoat* in the calm waters of Periwinkle Lagoon. As she looked out through the thick glass, her eyes feeling hot and teary, she thought she could see something moving amongst the red and purple trees. Something big.

"Wait," she said breathlessly, "I think I see . . ."

Marina's sentence was cut short by a terrifying bubbling roar that shook the capsulette and all inside it. The pirates felt the tentacles release their grip and the little vessel slowly settled on the seabed once more, surrounded by bubbles.

The three pirates sat in utter silence, not even daring to breathe. They waited for the bubbles to clear to reveal what had made the terrifying roar. And when they did, there in front of them in the dark forest . . . was the Nori.

Chapter Eight

"Quick," Aqua gasped, trying to compose herself, "release the net. We can easily catch her from here."

The Nori let out another loud roar, surrounding the capsulette in bubbles again.

"Limpets," said Oceana, "I can't see her now." Her finger was poised over the net release button.

"Wait," Marina interrupted, ushering Oceana not to press the button. "I think I see her, and I think she looks . . . hurt."

The bubbles cleared and revealed the Nori once again. She didn't appear as monstrous as Aqua's books had suggested – in fact, quite the opposite. She was indeed a large mermaid, but her teeth were perfect and pearly white, and instead of claws she had glittery green nails.

The three girls leant closer to look at the exquisite creature before them.

"Oh my," sighed Oceana, "the Nori is . . . "

" . . . beautiful," Marina finished her friend's sentence.

"I think you're right about her being hurt, Marina," said Aqua, pointing to the Nori's shimmering tail. "Look, it's cut."

The Nori, her long shimmery arms wrapped in pearls, gestured for the girls to follow her. Her long flaxen hair flowed behind her as she swam away.

"This might be a trick," Aqua said, her finger on her chin. "I'll bet you a billion barnacles that if we follow her, she'll lead us into her lair and eat us."

Oceana looked at Marina, her face as pale as a baby shark's belly.

"Well, Petticoat Pirates," Marina said, her head held high, "we came to capture the Nori and save Starfish Reef, and the Nori just went that way! We have to follow!"

Muttering a faint "limpets," Oceana reluctantly guided the capsulette through the Red Seaweed Forest, following the Nori.

Before long the forest opened out to reveal a clearing. In the centre stood a grand castle made from white coral. Its windows were framed with black pearls and its turrets were tiled with shiny mussel shells.

The Nori glided around the side of the castle to a large opening, shrouded by deep red seaweed, and swam through.

"It looks like the Nori wants us to follow her into that tunnel," Marina said.

"Yes, that dark, black, scary tunnel," Oceana replied, carefully steering the capsulette through the opening in the castle wall.

Gradually the tunnel sloped upward until the three pirates found themselves surfacing in a damp air-filled cavern. Marina opened the lid of the capsulette and stared in awe at her surroundings. The vaulted ceiling of the watery cave was completely covered with shiny white scallop shells, and a sparkling sea crystal chandelier gently lit up the room. Sitting on a pearl-encrusted chair was the Nori.

"I thought Captainess Periwinkle's ship was

fancy," Aqua gasped, "but this really takes the sea biscuit!"

Marina, Aqua and Oceana cautiously made their way up the coral steps towards the giant mermaid, who was squeezing seawater over her wound with a sponge.

"Perhaps we shouldn't go any closer," Oceana said nervously. "She IS a sea monster, after all."

"But she's clearly not a monster, Oceana," Marina replied. "It just proves that we shouldn't believe everything we hear about somebody before we've met them ourselves."

"My name is Marina," she began to speak in Mer, "and these are my friends Oceana and Aqua. We are the Petticoat Pirates."

As the Nori ushered the girls to move closer to her, Marina could see how badly

93

injured her tail was. She leant in towards the Nori, and heard the mermaid making a faint sound.

"I'm sssorry, I'm ssso very sssorry."

"Great gulls!" exclaimed Marina. "You speak . . ."

"Yesss," replied the Nori in a bubbling accent, "I ssspeak your language."

"Well, you've got some explaining to do," snapped Aqua, stepping in front of her two friends, her pretty blue eyes fixed firmly on the Nori.

"I know why you are so angry," the Nori continued, squeezing some more seawater over her wound. "There's been a terrible misunderstanding."

"Go on," Marina said.

"I'll ssstart at the beginning," said the

Nori. "It was a night much like any other and I was making my way up the reef towards the mer-farms in the reef's shallows. I love to swim around the mer-farms, but I have to go when all the mermaids are asleep so as not to frighten them. The rows of sea lettuce and sea cauliflowers are so pretty and they get bigger every time I visit!"

Marina was confused. "Then why did you destroy them all?"

"Well, every time I swim over I bring a little bag of Red Forest blossom to feed the sea snails. They adore it." The Nori looked away and wiped a tear from her eye. "It only grows down here in the deep, dark and lonely ocean floor."

"You're lonely . . ." Oceana said, her head tilted to one side.

"Oh yes, so very lonely," the Nori said as she looked straight into Oceana's sand-coloured eyes. "The sea snails are always so pleased to see me; I know they're just animals but they are my only friends."

"So where are they? Have you snail-napped them? Are they locked in a cavern down here somewhere?" Aqua asked.

"Oh no, I would never take them away from their home! I was making my way over to their pens that night when I noticed the gate had been left open and some of the snails were escaping. I was rushing about, trying to collect them all and put them back, when the moon disappeared behind a cloud and I was plunged into darkness."

"So the mer-farmers had left the gate open?" Marina said.

"Yes, but it was what I did that caused the destruction. I panicked in the dark and caught my tail on a giant eel tooth that was wedged in the side of the reef." The Nori gestured to her sore tail.

"That looks terribly painful," Marina said, gently touching the Nori's green, glittering scales.

"Anyway, the sharp pain caused me to thrash my tail around and before I knew it I had crushed the snail-pen walls. As the snails began to escape, they crushed the sea lettuce and cauliflowers. I panicked and tried to herd them back in but only caused more damage to the sugar kelp fields."

"But why didn't you stay and explain what had happened?" asked Marina.

"Because I would have just caused MORE panic. The mermaids are nervous creatures and the sight of me would have frightened them. And my tail was hurting so much, I just wanted to come home."

"I see," said Marina. She stood up and examined the Nori's wound more closely. "Your tail needs medicine. The mer-farmers have a garden where they grow healing sea herbs. We'll take you there."

"But I can't go back there, not after what I've done!" the Nori said in a panicked tone.

"Once the mermaids of Starfish Reef understand what happened, they will help you. Then, once your tail is better, you can help replant the crops," Oceana suggested.

"And I can work out the currents and figure out where the sea snails have been swept to. A mermaid of your size could easily swim out and recapture them, couldn't you?" Aqua asked.

"Well, yes, I suppose I could. I'll do anything to make up for the damage I've caused," the Nori said, looking a little brighter.

"Well then that's what we'll do!" Marina declared.

Chapter Nine

It was a sight to behold: the little round capsulette with its row of tiny white lights being trailed by a mermaid that was twice its size. The Nori's anxious expression seemed to soften as they neared the top of Starfish Reef, their way being lit by the thousands of tiny glowing starfish once more.

"I think it best if we speak to Dulsie, Buttonweed and Slokie alone before we go any further," suggested Marina to Aqua and Oceana.

She gestured through the capsulette window for the Nori to wait.

The giant mermaid agreed and huddled as best she could against the wall of the reef face while the Petticoat Pirates went to find their mermaid friends who had been waiting in the safety of their houses.

Oceana steered them towards the mermaid houses, which were little caves carved into the walls of the reef. Pinkish golden light was now streaming down through the water as the sun rose up slowly in the morning sky.

As the capsulette came to rest on the seabed in front of her house, Buttonweed was already up, tending her medicinal garden. Marina gestured that she wanted the mermaid to follow her up to the surface so they could talk, but Buttonweed's face suddenly fell.

"What's going on?" Oceana said, trying to see what Buttonweed was looking at.

The waters around them suddenly filled with angry-looking mermaids, some holding

narwhal horns, others brandishing giant lobster claws.

"Limpets," muttered Oceana. "Have we done something to upset everybody?"

"I don't think it's us they're pointing their horns at," said Marina. "I think they've spotted the Nori before we've had a chance to explain!"

"Oh, limpets, limpets, limpets, limpets! The Nori will just swim away again. She's too shy and frightened to face these angry mermaids," Oceana wailed.

"Just a mussely minute," said Aqua, lifting her eyepatch up on to her head. "Do my pirate eyes deceive me?"

Oceana turned the capsulette around and, instead of seeing the Nori and her tail disappearing over the edge of the reef, the pirates saw her bravely and calmly hovering in

the water, her hands outstretched in a friendly manner.

"That's my girl," Aqua said, punching the air with her fist.

"Oceana, can you turn on the listening device?" said Marina. "I want to hear what she says."

Oceana twiddled a little round button, and tapped the capsulette's speakers as they crackled into life.

"Mermaids of Starfish Reef," Marina translated the Nori's words for her friends. "Please do not be afraid, please do not be angry."

Slowly, the mermaids lowered their narwhal horns and lobster claws and listened. But they still looked suspicious.

"I've come here to Starfish Reef to help

you. I can round up your sea snail herds and replant your crops, but I need your help first."

"Flippers!" said Aqua, listening intently. "She's being so brave."

"Why should we help you? You destroyed our farms!" cried one of the mermaids.

"Wait, mermaids," interrupted Buttonweed. "Our friends the Petticoat Pirates have brought the Nori here. There must be a good reason why."

Marina nodded to Buttonweed through the thick glass, relieved.

"How do you need our help?" asked Slokie.

The Nori pointed to the deep cut and the eel tooth stuck in her tail.

"I need healing before I will have the strength to help you. The pirates tell me you have a medicinal garden."

"That's true," said Dulsie, "it was the one

garden that didn't get destroyed. We will help you, great Nori. But you must explain what happened."

"You are very kind mermaids," the Nori said in a soft voice. "I'll tell you everything."

After the Nori had told her story to the mermaids, Dulsie led Marina, Oceana and Aqua to the surface. The capsulette's lid hissed open and Dulsie handed them three sea crystal diving helmets and three long twirly shells.

"Put these helmets over your heads," she instructed, "and strap the shells to your backs. They are filled with air and will allow you to breathe underneath the water. You'll be able to join us in the ocean and swim around freely."

"Thank you, Dulsie," the three pirates said in unison, before pulling the helmets over their heads.

"I look ridiculous!" Aqua scoffed.

"Aqua," Marina laughed, "if anyone can carry off wearing a crystal helmet and an oversized shell on their back, it's you!"

"Come on," said Oceana. "Let's dive down before it's too late to see what's happening with the Nori."

Dulsie led the three girls to one of the larger cave houses.

Inside they found the Nori, who seemed even bigger than usual under the low ceilings!

Moments after they entered, Buttonweed came in carrying a little basket filled with sea herbs and a long frond of seaweed.

"Here," said Buttonweed, handing the Nori a small spray of bright pink sea flowers. "You must chew on these – they will help you to feel much better."

As the day passed, and the afternoon turned into evening, the mermaids treated the Nori's wound and she began to recover. The mermaids' fear of the Nori had disappeared. Now all they felt was sympathy and understanding.

"The sun is low in the sky now, girls," Slokie said to Marina in Mer. "You must return to the surface before the air in your shells runs out."

Then Marina translated as Buttonweed spoke to the girls.

"Thank you for your bravery and for

solving the mystery of how our farms were destroyed. The Nori will be well enough to help us replant tomorrow after she has had a good night's rest. We would like to thank you by way of a feast tomorrow evening at Periwinkle Lagoon." Buttonweed took out a rolled-up piece of flat seaweed. "Please also pass this note on to Captainess Periwinkle."

Marina took the seaweed, which was tied with a little frond of pink lace weed, and tucked it under her arm. The three girls hugged the four mermaids then swam up to the surface to *The Petticoat*.

"Aaaah," sighed Aqua as she wrung out her skirt over the edge of the ship. "It's good to be back on board."

"As much as I loved the underwater wonderland of Starfish Reef, I much prefer

my own cosy cabin," laughed Oceana. She had already taken off her shoes and was pouring out the seawater.

"Well," said Marina, "if we set sail now, we'll make it back to Periwinkle Lagoon by dawn. Let's get out of these wet clothes and get going!"

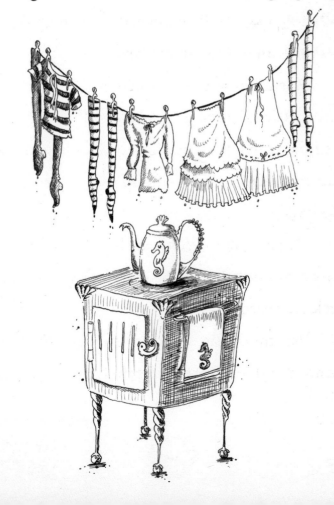

"Aye, aye, Capt'n!" Aqua and Oceana shouted in unison.

As the wood burner crackled away in the corner of the cabin, drying their clothes, the girls sailed back towards Periwinkle Lagoon in their pyjamas. They couldn't wait to tell Captainess Periwinkle all about their adventure and the upcoming celebration feast!

Chapter Ten

Periwinkle Lagoon was buzzing with news of the Petticoat Pirates' victorious mission. Everybody was very relieved to hear that the Nori wasn't a terrifying sea monster, but a lonely and misunderstood mermaid.

"I'm as proud as a whale," Captainess Periwinkle declared as she hugged her three pirate girls on the deck of *The Petticoat*.

Marina handed the Captainess the seaweed message from Buttonweed.

"The mermaids will be arriving with the Nori at sundown. I'll arrange for the glowing jellyfish to be lined up to light their way. And we'd better set up the feasting floats. May the festivities commence!" called the Captainess. Then she disappeared over the edge of *The Petticoat* to organise the rest of the pirates.

After a busy day of preparation, Marina looked out over the lagoon as the sun began to set. The feasting floats' masts were decorated with acres of bunting and there were strings of glowing starfish draped from float to float.

Slowly the tables filled up with hungry pirates, all ready for a hearty pirate feast.

"How do I look?" Aqua said as she clomped out of her cabin, swirling her pink net skirt around her and doing a little curtsey.

"You look fabulous," said Marina. "I especially like the hat."

"You don't think it's too much?" Aqua asked, adjusting the large stuffed seagull on top of her gold sequinned hat.

"For you? Nothing's too much!" Marina laughed.

"Are we ready then?" said a little voice from behind Oceana's cabin door.

"Yes, are *you* ready, Oceana?

Let's have a look at you then!" Marina called back.

Shyly, Oceana shuffled out, her mother-of-pearl-rimmed glasses staring down at her sea crystal high-heeled sandals.

"Blinking barnacles, Oceana," Aqua cried aloud, "you look beautiful!"

"Thank you," Oceana managed to

mutter. "I finished sewing the sea sequins on this afternoon."

"It's the prettiest dress I've ever seen! It makes this old thing look like a sea hag's hand-me-downs!" Marina said, pulling at her silken green full skirt and her bodice of woven seaweed.

"Well, neither of you look as good as me, so let's just go!" joked Aqua. The three pirates climbed down *The Petticoat*'s hull and into their little rowing boat.

"Over here!" called Captainess Periwinkle as they moored by the floats. "You three will take pride of place next to me at the Captainess's table!"

Marina, Oceana and Aqua sat down, beaming.

"Look!" cried Captainess Periwinkle. "Here they come!"

All the pirates in Periwinkle Lagoon twisted around to look at the entrance to the lagoon. Swimming along the surface of the water was a long line of mermaids all carrying trays of colourful seafood delights.

The Nori, Buttonweed, Slokie and Dulsie were at the front of the line. The pirates all cheered and clapped as the mermaids laid plate after plate of scrumptious food on the

tables. There were bright red and pink shiny prawns, plates of deep crimson lobster and purple spotty fried octopus! There

were fish of every size and

flavour, all beautifully garnished
with seaweeds and seashells.

There was even sugar
kelp punch for the
pirates' seashell cups.

The last four
mermaids to enter the
lagoon were carrying
an enormous tray on
which was balanced the biggest cake anyone
had ever seen! It was in the shape of the Nori
and the body was made from carved sugared
sea sponge. Her tail was formed of hundreds
of slices of sugared sea cucumber and her hair
was sea spaghetti!

The pirates erupted with cheers and
squeals of delight.

"Pirates and mermaids alike!" shouted

Captainess Periwinkle. She stood up from her chair, her beautiful pearl necklaces swinging from side to side. "Please raise your seashell cups to these three brave pirates!"

The Captainess gestured for the girls to stand up.

"Marina, Aqua and Oceana are three of the truest and bravest pirates ever to exist! With their skills and with the help of the kind mermaids at Starfish Reef, they have solved the mystery of the sea monster and discovered a new friend in the Nori!"

Marina held her two friends' hands tightly and smiled at them in turn. "I couldn't have done any of this without you," she whispered.

"Likewise," Aqua and Oceana whispered back.

"May the Petticoat Pirates prevail!" shouted Captainess Periwinkle.

"Petticoat Pirates prevail!" shouted the pirates of Periwinkle Lagoon in unison.

"So," Marina winked at her friends as she held up her cup of sugar kelp punch, "until our next adventure?"

The three Petticoat Pirates clinked their cups together. "Until then!" the friends whispered. For there was always another adventure waiting around the corner.

The End

Ship's Log

Now that you've learnt all about Marina,
Aqua and Oceana, why not read on to see
how you can have a Petticoat Pirate
adventure of your own!

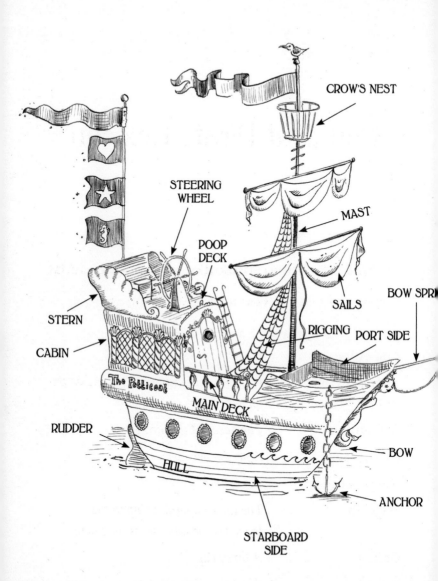

CROW'S NEST

STEERING
WHEEL

POOP
DECK

MAST

STERN

SAILS

BOW SPRI

CABIN

RIGGING   PORT SIDE

The Petticoat

MAIN DECK

RUDDER

HULL

BOW

ANCHOR

STARBOARD
SIDE

Petticoat Pirate Lexicon

Would you like to speak like a proper Petticoat Pirate? Of course you would!

Ahoy there!	*Hello!*
Anchors aweigh!	*It's time to raise the anchor and go on an adventure!*
Captainess	*The queen of the pirates*
Cartographer	*A person who draws maps*
Come hither	*Come here*
Flagship	*The most important ship in the lagoon – the Captainess lives here*
Goblet	*A fancy cup*
Kelp tea	*A delicious hot drink made from an underwater plant*

Kelp punch	*A sweet, cold drink made from the same plant!*
Limpets!	*Oh no!*
Me hearty	*This is what you should call your fellow pirates*
Morn	*Morning*
My little catfish	*A lovely thing to call a clever and nice person (you can also say "you're as clever as a catfish's whiskers")*
Nipper	*Very young pirate*
Port	*Left*
Starboard	*Right*
Sugared sea sponge	*A yummy snack*

May the Petticoat Pirates prevail!

We wish the Petticoat Pirates strength and success!

Make Your Own Petticoat Pirate Eyepatch

This is the perfect activity for rainy days. With your own eyepatch you can look exactly like a Petticoat Pirate! (You might need a little bit of help from a grown-up for this activity.)

What you will need

- A piece of elastic (you could adjust our instructions to use ribbon or string instead)

- A piece of scrap paper or card to draw your eyepatch shape onto

- Coloured felt (or thick paper or card)

- Scissors

- Glue

- Any decorations you like – for example sequins, glitter, beads or ribbon

What to do

1. You need to decide the shape of your eyepatch. Will you make a heart-shape like Marina? Or a star-shape like Aqua? Perhaps you'd prefer to make up your own shape!

2. Draw your shape onto the scrap paper/card and cut it out. Make sure that it's big enough to cover your eye!

3. Use this as a template to cut out the shape from your piece of felt. Cut two little slits, one on each side of the shape.

4. Measure your elastic so that it is long enough to circle your head. Then thread the elastic through the slits and tie the ends together.

5. Finally, add your decorations! Using glue or thread, make your eyepatch sparkly and beautiful.

6. Now you're ready to be a Petticoat Pirate!

Decorate a Nori

Use this image to draw and decorate your own Nori! You can trace or copy the image and then use whatever materials you like to decorate. We suggest lots of glitter!